George and the Big Red Fish

By Beth Clark

Illustrated by Jason Velázquez

George and the Big Red Fish
© 2020 by Beth Clark
Illustrated by Jason Velazquez

Printed in the United States of America.
ISBN-13: 978-1-7353862-2-5
LCCN: 2020920894

Beth Books
Blackshear, Georgia

beth
BOOKS

Hi! My name is George, and I am 8 years old. This is MY STORY--just as I told it to my grams.

My dad took me fishing this summer--it was different than our usual fishing in fresh water.

Dad and I went to the beach at the ocean. We got on a boat with a captain--just Dad and I.

The first thing we had to do was put on a life jacket and get some rules about being on a boat.

As we were going out, we took a large net to catch baitfish. There was a big basket for those fish. No worms or crickets here. Then we cut up the fish for bait--pieces about five inches long. I liked helping with the bait.

Then we went into deeper water. We tried several places until we found a good spot and it was a good one! The captain threw the lines. All we had to do was reel in a fish after we hooked it. I could not see a fish until I reeled it close enough to the boat to net it.

My fishing pole was not like when we freshwater fished, but similar. It was bigger and stronger. The captain would put the cut bait on the hook for us.

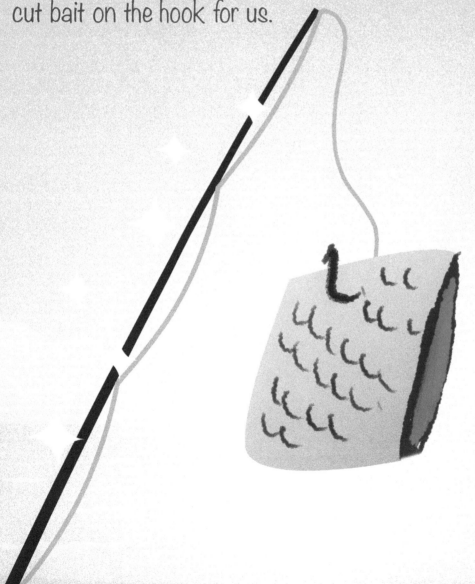

Dad and I did well. Dad caught the first fish, which was a toadfish, which was not good to eat. I caught the first good-to-eat fish, which was a whiting--very good. Between Dad and I, we caught 20 to 30 whiting, and all together, more than 50 fish!

The captain explained the different kinds of fish. We caught whiting, snapper, sheep's head, tartan, and of course, redfish. We also caught a saltwater catfish, which they called "trash fish." There were lots of different kinds.

As we were fishing, something amazing happened!! A stingray jumped out of the water and flipped over and back into the water. The captain told us that stingrays would swim as fast as they can into a big school of baitfish to catch their food. He said it was unusual for a stingray to jump up like that, and you would probably only see that once in a lifetime!!

When Big Red bit down, the rod went down, and I started reeling and trying to keep the rod from being pulled into the water. Dad helped, keeping the rod from getting away, and I reeled him in.

He probably weighed about 30 pounds. This trip was one of most exciting things in my life.

The captain and Dad helped me get Big Red off the hook and let me hold him while they took pictures.

The only bad thing was that I could not keep Big Red. I learned that there are rules about how big or little a fish is that lets you know if you can keep a fish. Some are too small and some too big. We had to throw lots of our catches back into the ocean.

Big Red had to go back into the water, but I will remember him for a long, long time. We are going to go fishing again on this boat, and maybe I will see Big Red again.

My favorite part of this trip was being with my dad, but I also liked reeling in the big fish and cutting up the bait. Maybe you will one day be able to go fishing!!!

Also by Beth Clark

TOBY
THE GOPHER TURTLE

BY BETH CLARK
ILLUSTRATED BY JASON VELAZQUEZ

CPSIA information can be obtained
at www.ICGtesting.com
Printed in the USA
LVHW072229211120
672149LV00022B/507